Events of the Revolution

The Fall
of the Quaker City

By Susan & John Lee

Illustrated by Richard Wahl

 CHILDRENS PRESS, CHICAGO

Library of Congress Cataloging in Publication Data

Lee, Susan.
    The fall of the Quaker City.

    (Events of the Revolution)
    SUMMARY: A Quaker family in Pennsylvania must
decide whether or not to support the Revolution.
    [1. United States—History—Revolution, 1775-1783—
Fiction. 2. Philadelphia—Fiction. 3. Friends,
Society of—Fiction] I. Lee, John, joint author.
II. Wahl, Richard, 1939- ill. III. Title.
PZ7.L51487Fal   [Fic]   74-23343
ISBN 0-516-04672-1

2 3 4 5 6 7 8 9 10 11 12 R 78 77 76 75

Chapter 1
A NOISY FOURTH OF JULY

Ting-a-ling.

Sarah heard the bell and ran to the front of the shop.

"Good afternoon, Mrs. Swanson," said Sarah.

"Today is a holiday," said the old lady. "Is the bakery open?"

"Yes, it's open. What would thee like?" said Sarah.

"A loaf of bread," said Mrs. Swanson.

Sarah put the bread in her neighbor's basket. She was ten years old, but she knew how to add a bill and make change.

"We're taking a picnic supper down to the river," said Mrs. Swanson. "We will watch the boats and then the parade. Would you like to come with us?"

Sarah's father came into the front room. His face was red from the heat of the ovens.

"Sarah thanks thee for thy kindness," the baker said, "but she must help me. Today is not a holiday in our house."

He wiped his hands on a floury apron as if to say 'that's final'.

"But Father," said Sarah. "It's been one year since Congress declared independence. Everyone in Philadelphia is taking the day off."

"Not everyone," replied her father. "There are many others like us who find no reason to celebrate the fourth of July. The holiday is just a way to get people all excited about fighting. In this house, we honor God, not war."

"Mr. Miller! How can you say such things with your son off fighting for General Washington?" said Mrs. Swanson.

"We do not speak of Thomas in this house," answered the baker. "He is no longer a Quaker and has chosen to disobey his family."
Mr. Miller held the door for his neighbor.

"At least leave candles in your window tonight," advised Mrs. Swanson. "If you don't, you will be in danger."

Mr. Miller shook his head as he closed the shop door. "Mrs. Swanson always has advice."

"She means well," said Sarah.

"Sarah, Sarah! Would thee please set the table?" called her mother.

Sarah hurried into the back parlor and began helping her mother get ready for supper.

"Mother," said Sarah. "Why can't we see the fireworks tonight? We don't have to clap or cheer. We can just watch."

"Did thee not hear what thy father said?" answered her mother. "War only brings hardship and suffering to people. Thee must learn that to love God thee must love man."

"But Mother! I do. I love thee and Father. I love Thomas. And Thomas is fighting for our independence."

"Sarah!" Mr. Miller had come into the parlor. "That is enough. Thee must go to thy room and think about what thy mother said. When thee understands, thee may come down for supper."

Sarah knew better than to argue with her father. She climbed up the ladder to her bedroom in the loft.

It was no use trying to read. Sarah thought about Thomas, and the day he had left to join the American Army.

"I will miss thee so much, Thomas," she had said, trying not to cry.

"Here now," he had said, giving her a big hug. "Will thee take care of my things while I am away?" he asked.

"Oh, yes," Sarah replied. "Is it all right if I read thy books, too?"

"Of course," he had answered. Then he kissed her good-bye and disappeared down the ladder.

Where was he now? Sarah wondered.

Hours later Sarah heard bells ringing, then the bang-pop-pop of fireworks. Looking out the window she could barely see the beautiful display of lights.

Sarah leaned out further. Then, slowly and carefully, she put a leg over the windowsill. Soon she was sitting on the roof watching the fireworks. The sky looked like a garden of wild flowers.

Sarah heard the loud rap of shoes on the cobblestones. She did not want to lean too far over to see what all the noise was about.

"Look! There's no candles in that window," she heard a voice shout.

"Miller's Bakery," cried another.

"He must be a Tory," said another.

"A Quaker. He's a Quaker," said a voice Sarah knew. It was a boy who lived in Cooper's Court.

"Well, let's show these Quakers what independence is all about," said the ringleader.

Crash! Sarah heard a rock go through the shop window. The gang of boys cheered.

Crash! Another window broke.

Sarah got down low on the roof and began crawling back towards the window.

"Look!" cried one of the boys. "There's a little sissy Quaker on the roof. She's running away. That's what they all do."

Everyone laughed, then they began to shout:

"Quaker, Quaker,
Inner light,
Tells you not to
Stand and fight."

Sarah crawled back into the loft and climbed down the ladder. There was glass all over the front room. Mr. Miller was calmly sweeping it up.

"I understand what thee means," she said to her father. "War just makes people act mean."

Mr. Miller smiled. "It's late," he said. "Aren't thee hungry for some supper?"

Chapter 2
RECESS FROM SCHOOL

Summer was over, school had begun. Sarah liked the new teacher.

"Now," said Brother Todd, "the last word to spell today is 'grammar'." The teacher banged on his desk for the students to start. The class began to spell out loud together:

"G-r-a-m-m". . .a few voices dropped out towards the end.

"Martha!" Mr. Todd barked. "Spell 'grammar'."

Martha stood up and slowly began to spell: "G-r-a-m-m. . .e-r."

"I thought so. Martha, take Fox's Speller and look up the right spelling. Then write 'grammar' ten times in thy copybook."

Martha sat down in shame and began to leaf through her speller.

"Now, everyone, again, spell 'grammar'." He hit his desk with a strap.

"G-r-a-m-m-a-r." This time the voices were loud and clear.

"All right. Now get out thy pen, ink, and copybooks."

Sarah sighed. How she hated penmanship.

"Turn to page 14. This is the lesson I told thee to practice at home. I want thee to copy it into thy book without a mistake. And remember not to crowd thy words together on thy page."

Sarah turned to page 14 and began to write:

"Thirty days hath September,
April, June, and November."

Scratch, scratch. The room was quiet except for the sound of everyone copying.

Sarah looked out the window. The September day was very warm. She set her pen down quietly and slipped one of Thomas' books out from under her skirts. It fit neatly inside her penmanship book. Sarah found her place and began reading.

Scratch, scratch. Sarah forgot all about penmanship.

Suddenly she felt a kick, but the warning came too late. Mr. Todd took the book from her hands.

"Well, what have we here? A pupil who would rather read Thomas Paine's *Common Sense* than do penmanship lessons."

Sarah felt her face grow red with shame.

"Sarah. What kind of book is this for a young lady to be reading? Do thy parents know thee hast this book?"

"No, sir," replied Sarah.

"I thought not," said Mr. Todd. "Just listen to what this man Thomas Paine has to say," and he began reading to the class:

"The principles of Quakerism have a direct tendency to make a man the quiet subject of any and every government which is set over him."

Everyone stared at Sarah in disbelief. Sarah kept her eyes on her desk.

Mr. Todd was not done. He flipped over a few pages and read out loud again:

"In short, independence is the only bond that can tie and keep us together."

"Well, it is just as well that thee heard what Thomas Paine had to say. It is always difficult for Quakers in time of war. But thee must remember that independence cannot tie us together. Only love and understanding can do that."

Sarah's head began to hurt. Mr. Todd went on.

"Today, I am sorry to say, is our last day of class. The school must close because I will not swear loyalty to the new state of Pennsylvania."

He leaned forward on his desk. "As thee well know, I am loyal to God, and God alone. As a Quaker, I cannot swear an oath to anyone but Him. I hope school will open again soon. But for now thee may go home."

After the other girls had left, Sarah stayed behind to tell Brother Todd she was sorry. When she came outside, her friend Mary was waiting.

"Did thee get thy book back?" asked Mary.

"Yes, I told him it belonged to Thomas." The two began walking up Fourth Steeet, then turned on Chestnut.

"Just think," said Mary. "No more school. What shall we do tomorrow?"

"I'll probably have to help in the bakery, just like I do when school's out," answered Sarah.

The two girls passed a hat shop.

"Look at that bonnet," said Mary. "The pink one with ribbons. I wonder how much it costs?"

"I like the blue one with flowers," said Sarah. "Maybe someday we won't have to wear these dull gray bonnets."

"Come on," said Mary. "Let's cut up Strawberry Alley. I'm supposed to buy a *Pennsylvania Gazette* on the way home from school."

They passed the Bull's Head Tavern and crossed Market Street to B. Franklin's Printing Office. An apprentice in a brown leather apron was setting type as the girls came inside.

"What may I do for you today?" he asked.

"Please, sir, I wish to buy today's *Gazette*," said Mary.

The apprentice smiled and reached for a copy. "Here you are. It looks like the British may have Washington's army trapped."

Mary paid the apprentice, and the girls headed up Second Street for home.

"What else does it say?" asked Sarah. "My father won't read the *Gazette* because it favors independence."

"Look," said Mary. "Right here it says the Quaker leaders are a danger to the new state of Pennsylvania. It says these men must sign an oath as proof of their loyalty."

"I wonder what will happen if they don't sign?" said Sarah.

"I don't know," answered Mary. "But look what happened to Brother Todd. He can't be a teacher. He lost his job. It's just not fair."

"Maybe we'll find out more at Sunday meeting," said Sarah.

Chapter 3
A QUAKER GOLDEN RULE

Everything in the meeting house was very quiet.

Sarah looked at her father across the room. He was deep in thought.

It was warm in the room. Sarah wished she could take off her bonnet. She looked at the elders. They sat on raised benches at the front, facing the other church members.

Brother Smith crossed his leg.

Someone coughed.

Outside a cart rolled over the cobblestones.

Sarah thought about Thomas. Was he safe? If Washington was fighting to keep the British from entering Philadelphia, then maybe Thomas was close by.

Suddenly the quiet ended. Someone behind Sarah began to speak. Sarah could tell from the voice that it was Sister Griscom, who lived around the corner.

"These are difficult times for Quakers. As we all know, some of our dear Friends have been taken from their families and made prisoners because they will not sign the loyalty oath. We have protested to the Council. But our protests have not done any good. On Thursday they will be sent under guard to Virginia until the war is over. I feel that this action is very unjust, and if the British take Philadelphia, I will support them."

She sat down.

Then Mary's father got up. Brother Porter spoke calmly, but his cheeks were very red.

"I cannot agree with Sister Griscom. God teaches us to love all men. War makes this very difficult. But we must stay out of this fight all

together, and that means we cannot favor either side."

Brother Porter sat down.

Then one of the elders stood up. He had bright blue eyes. It seemed to Sarah as if he could always tell when she wasn't paying attention.

Brother Allen spoke in gentle tones.

"This is no time for Quakers to disagree among themselves. We have done all we could to keep our Friends from being sent to Virginia. Now we must help their families. While these men are away, it is up to us to comfort their wives and children."

Brother Allen stopped to clear his throat. Then he went on:

"As for the war, it looks as though General Washington will try to stop General Howe from taking Philadelphia. Many men will probably be hurt in the fighting. We must remember to be a friend to anyone in need. Love must be our golden rule at all times."

The elder sat down. For a long time all was quiet. Then Brother Allen shook hands with Brother Porter and the meeting was over.

Outside, Sarah and Mary listened to the news. Everyone was talking about whether the British would take Philadelphia.

"Thee can see why Howe decided to march into Pennsylvania," Mr. Miller was saying. "Philadelphia is the capital of all the colonies. What a feather in British caps if they can win this city."

"Thee can be sure if they do, it will mean suffering for everyone, most of all for the poor," Mr. Porter added.

"I understand Washington has taken his army south of the city, near Wilmington," said Mr. Miller.

"What chance has he of stopping Howe's men? Did thee see that rag-tag American army when Washington marched it through town? These rebels haven't got a chance against trained soldiers." Mr. Porter shook his head.

"Well, no doubt if there is a battle, that will be the end of Washington. The war will be over in a week," said the baker hopefully.

The Millers and Porters began walking home.

"Hast thou heard anything from Thomas?" Mrs. Porter asked.

"Not yet," said Sarah. "But we will. He'll let us know he's safe as soon as he can."

"Sarah!" her father interrupted. "Sarah does not understand," explained Mr. Miller. "Thomas chose war over his Quaker beliefs. For that he has been read out of meeting. For all I know, when he decided to join the American Army, he left home forever."

"That's not true," cried Sarah. "He'll be back. He said he would." She felt tears fill her eyes.

"There, there." Mrs. Miller put her arm around Sarah. "Let's talk about something besides war."

"Like no more school," said Mary.

"Just because school is closed doesn't mean thy education is over," said Mrs. Porter. "Perhaps it would be a good idea if I spent some time every day going over lessons with thee and Sarah. How would thee like that?"

The two girls smiled with excitement.

"Our own school! Just for the two of us! Thee can hear our spelling and give us sums to figure," said Mary.

"And we can take turns reading out loud for thee," Sarah added. "What fun!"

"A wonderful idea, Sister Porter," said Mrs. Miller. "I shall be glad to help."

"And there's no better time to start than today," said Mr. Miller. "Sarah, how would thee like to begin by doing the Bible readings this afternoon?"

Sarah nodded. The more she had to do, the faster time would pass. And the faster time passed, the sooner Thomas would be back home.

Chapter 4
BAD NEWS FROM BRANDYWINE

"Come on, Peg. Today is Market Day and we're going!" Sarah talked to the horse as she hitched Old Peg to the wagon.

The sun had not been up for long, but Second Street was already noisy with people. Next door, Mrs. Swanson was sweeping the sidewalk hard enough to make the cracks disappear. Abraham, the blacksmith's apprentice, was buying firewood from a peddler. Up and down the street, housewives with baskets hurried about their daily shopping. Already, customers were coming into Miller's Bakery.

"Are thee ready, Sarah?" asked her father. "Doest thou have the money?"

"Yes, Father. After waiting all week to go to market, I wouldn't forget anything."

Mr. Miller led Old Peg south and turned onto Market Street. The clang of iron wheels on the cobblestones made a huge noise. Sarah jumped out of the wagon so she could look at the displays.

"Look!" she cried to her father. "Raisins and nutmeg! Doesn't the chocolate look good!"

"Look at the cost instead," fussed her father. "Who ever heard of chocolate at 5 shillings a pound? Ever since this war with England began, prices have gone up like a kite. We'll be lucky just to buy enough flour for the bakery."

"It doesn't cost to look, Father," Sarah answered.

Stalls of apples and berries caught her eye. Chickens and mutton hung from hooks in one shed. Farmers were selling corn and apple cider from the back of their wagons. Sarah hoped there would be a few pennies left over to buy some pumpkin for a pie.

"Sarah, Sarah!" she heard voices call. It was Hans and Peter with Mr. Schmidt. A crowd of customers clustered around their stall.

"Good day, Mr. Schmidt," said Sarah's father shaking hands with the farmer.

"Mr. Miller, *guten morgen.* I was afraid you would not come." Mr. Schmidt spoke in a thick German accent.

"Good morning, Mr. Schmidt," said Sarah. "My father and I need to buy six sacks of flour for the bakery."

"Ach!" said Mr. Schmidt. "I have bad news. It is only three sacks I was able to bring you.

Soldiers have been raiding farms to feed the American Army. Just this week, my neighbor had all his potatoes taken with nothing but promises to pay. How can we farmers live on promises?"

"Yes, this war has upset everything. It is driving prices way up. I am grateful to thee for the three sacks of flour thee did bring," said Mr. Miller.

"I am sorry the flour has gone up so much in price. From one week to the next, the cost is never the same," said Mr. Schmidt.
"Sarah," said her father, "we must pay Mr. Schmidt and finish our shopping."

Sarah took out some coins and counted them slowly into Mr. Schmidt's hand. He gave her only a few pennies back.

"Hans! Peter! Put Mr. Miller's order into the cart."

The boys began at once to put the heavy sacks of flour into the baker's wagon.

"Many thanks, Mr. Schmidt. I hope to see thee next week."

"It may be a long time before we meet again, Mr. Miller. Out in Germantown, they are saying that Howe will take Philadelphia with no trouble. If that happens, Washington will try to starve the British into giving up."

"And starve us all as well," said Mr. Miller. "But let us hope that does not happen."

The two men shook hands.

Mr. Miller pulled on Old Peg. "Now," he said, "we need some salt and then we'll head for home."

"But Father," said Sarah. "Can't we buy something for Mother?"

"Perhaps next week," he said. "The flour cost more than I planned, and we must have salt."

By now the streets were jammed with shoppers. A pig was loose, and its owner was pushing through the crowds trying to catch it.

Mr. Miller stopped at several stalls. At each place he received the same answer.

"I am sorry, but I have no salt to sell at any price."

"Father, why is everyone out of salt?" Sarah asked.

"It is one of those things everyone wants in time of war. No doubt the soldiers have taken most of it. Perhaps we will have more luck on the waterfront."

Mr. Miller led Old Peg towards the Fish Market.

Sarah loved the sounds and smells of the river. There were always so many strange-looking people down by the docks.

"Father, where do all the sailors come from?"
she asked.

"Why, lots of places, Sarah. The West Indies.
France. Even the Orient. We buy tea, sugar, and
spices from them, and they buy meat, furs, and
wood from us."

Mr. Miller began looking for salt. Always he
got the same answer.

"No salt today!"

Suddenly there was shouting across the street.
A soldier on horseback was riding up to the
London Coffee House. Mr. Miller pulled Old
Peg across Front Street so he could hear the
news. Everyone else had the same idea. Soon a
huge crowd pressed around the rider.

"General Howe has attacked Washington at
Brandywine Creek. The American Army has
retreated to Chester. The road to Philadelphia is
wide open!"

Everyone began talking at once.

"Does this mean the Redcoats are heading this
way?" a man shouted.

"We have every reason to think so," answered the rider. "By order of the Council, all shops and stores are to be closed immediately. Every man capable of bearing arms must report to his captain's quarters at two, this afternoon. And we need boats to bring the wounded back to Philadelphia."

Sarah wanted to know if Thomas was safe.

"Ask him how soon before we know about the wounded," she whispered to her father.

"No, child. It is too soon for that. Come, we must hurry home and tell thy mother this latest news."

Chapter 5
A CLOSE CALL FOR CONGRESS

"Good-bye!"

"Take care!"

"Look out!"

"Giddap!"

"So long!"

Sarah woke to the sound of noisy shouting in the street below. She looked out the window, but it was too dark to see.

Sarah dressed quickly and went downstairs. She found her father in the kitchen, preparing the ovens for the day's baking.

"Sarah! What are thee doing up so early?"

"I heard the noise, Father. What's going on?" Sarah began to put on her coat.

"I don't know," he replied. "If thee goes out I want thee back here in ten minutes. No longer. Do thee hear?"

Sarah heard, so she rushed all the more. Outside, the street was full of people packing their belongings in carts. Animals crowded the streets. Everything was noise and haste.

Across the street, she spotted Abraham the apprentice drawing water from the public pump.

"What's happening?" she cried.

"The British are coming!" he shouted. "People who want independence are leaving town before they get here."

"How doest thou know?" she replied.

"Well," he shouted back, "Congress is moving the capital to Lancaster."

Sarah didn't wait for more news. She cut through the Quaker cemetery, crossed Market Street, and ran down Petty's Alley to Fifth Street.

All along the way, Sarah saw that Abraham was right. Representatives of the 13 colonies were preparing to leave.

Servants ran in and out of rooming houses carrying baggage. Groups of people stood around watching their leaders escape.

Sarah went up to a man saddling his horse.

"Excuse me," said Sarah. "Why are the members of Congress leaving Philadelphia?"

"To save the government," he said with anger. "Congress can no longer count on Washington for protection. General Howe will bring his troops into the city any day now. So we must make Lancaster the capital. They are moving the Declaration of Independence to safety right now."

"I wish thee a safe trip, sir," Sarah replied and ran across Chestnut Street to the State House. The hands in the clock tower had not reached six.

In spite of the hour, Sarah saw several men coming through the huge carved doorway. They carried a trunk slowly down three stairs and lifted it into a waiting cart.

"Is that the Declaration of Independence?" Sarah heard a bystander ask.

"The Declaration and all the records of Congress," said one of the men. "The British will never get their hands on these papers."

Sarah turned. Some men were struggling to get the Liberty Bell into an open wagon.

"Come on," huffed one. "Lift."

The men walked a few steps, then stopped to rest.

"I don't care if the bloody British get this bell or not," said one. "I think we need more men to help us."

"Who cares what you think?" said a tall, red-haired man. "Do you know how many bullets the British could make from this bell? Hundreds. Now lift."

Sarah remembered a year ago, when she had been part of a large crowd who heard John Nixon read the the Declaration of Independence. Everyone had cheered, and the Liberty Bell had rung to their shouts of approval. No one had dreamed of the danger they would all soon face.

Sarah left the struggling men, walked up Fifth Street, and crossed Arch. By now, the streets were jammed with wagons heading for Lancaster Road.

Sarah rushed into the bakery, eager to report her news. But the sight of two soldiers talking to her father cooled her excitement.

"By order of General Washington," the soldier in charge was saying, "we must ask you for any blankets and carpets you have. They are needed for the army."

"I am sorry," her father replied. "I do not favor war. I can do nothing to help thee."

"Then, sir, we must search your house."

"Hast thou a search warrant?" asked Mr. Miller.

"Surely, sir, you understand. In times of war there are no rules. Now, if you'll stand aside, I'm afraid we'll have to take what we need."

Mr. Miller stood aside. The men disappeared into the back rooms. In a few minutes they returned carrying several blankets and Mr. Miller's heavy winter coat.

"Thee must not take my father's coat," said Sarah angrily.

"And *thee* had better learn that Quakers cannot sit on the fence forever," answered the soldier in charge. "Sooner or later, you'll have to favor one side or the other."

"We do!" said Sarah. "We favor independence. My brother is fighting with General Washington."

Both soldiers laughed. "Is he now? Well, in that case, we'll see that he gets your father's coat." They banged the door on the way out.

"Sarah," Mr. Miller's voice was firm. "It is time for breakfast."

Sarah reported her news as the family ate biscuits and porridge.

"And, so," finished Sarah, "it looks as if the British will really be coming into the city. What doest thou think of that?"

"I think," said Mrs. Miller, "that thee was gone much too long this morning. From now on, I want thee to stay around home."

Chapter 6
THE FALL OF PHILADELPHIA

"This dress is getting too small for me," said Sarah. "Maybe it would fit thee."

"It is short," answered Mary. "But no one will notice today."

The two girls were getting dressed, but neither one had slept a wink all night.

"Just think," said Mary. "Today, September 26, 1777, the British will take over the capital of the colonies."

"I half thought they would come in the middle of the night," answered Sarah. "To sneak in when everyone was asleep."

The two girls climbed down the ladder and began helping Mrs. Miller with breakfast.

"Well, good morning." She kissed the two girls. "Did thee finally go to sleep last night?"

"With Father out on patrol?" Sarah asked.

Just then Mr. Miller and Mr. Porter entered the parlor.

"Well, another night without any fires. But I never heard so many stories." Mr. Miller dropped into a chair.

"Well, people have reason to be afraid," said Mr. Porter. "One patrol did arrest two men. They confessed that they had plans to set the city on fire."

"Oh no!" said Mrs. Miller. "What next?"

"Now remain calm," said Mr. Miller. "General Howe sent word to the people of Philadelphia yesterday. He said if everyone remained quietly in their homes, no one would get hurt."

"Well, after being out all night, I hast better let thy mother know I'm safe. She'll want to hear all the news. Mary Porter, thee may stay here, but do whatever Brother Miller says."

Mary's father let himself out the front door, and everyone sat down for breakfast. Mr. Miller said the blessing.

"Is it true," asked Sarah, "that the British will march down Second Street?"

"That's what I understand," said her father. "And if they do, I don't want either of thee to set foot outside this house."

"Can we look out the window?" asked Mary.

"Girls, girls," said Mrs. Miller. "There is so much work to be done. I think thee. . ."

She stopped. Everyone stopped. The sound of music was clear. Mary and Sarah ran to the front room and looked out the store window.

"Look!" said Sarah. "Men on horses!"

Down Second Street came rows and rows of soldiers on horseback. Their bright swords danced in the morning sun.

"And here comes the band," said Mary.

"They're playing *God Save The King*," shouted Sarah. "I bet the people on Pine Street can hear it."

Behind the band came foot soldiers. They marched in time to the music. The troops seemed to go on and on. Another band. More soldiers. Cannon. Baggage wagons. Even cows and goats. At last it was over.

"Now, Sarah, get thy books. Thee and Mary have wasted enough time. Sister Porter has probably been waiting all morning to hear thy lessons."

Sarah gathered up her books.

"And Sarah," added Mr. Miller, "Thee are going straight to Mary's. Is that clear?"

"Thee knows we will, Father," answered Sarah.

The two girls walked down Second Street, then crossed over to Mary's.

"Look, Mary, across the street. It's one of the British officers."

"He's staying at the St. George and the Dragon Inn! Think of it, we're going to have British soldiers right in our block!"

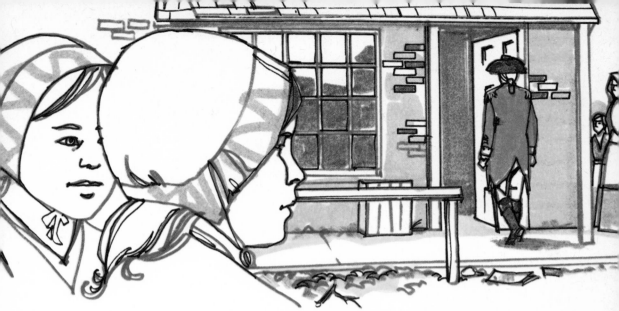

"Well, they have to stay somewhere. Father says some of the officers are going to move into rich people's homes."

"What a good chance to spy," said Mary. "The officers probably know everything that's going on."

"Mary! Thou hast given me an idea. I bet that man knows how we can find out the names of wounded men."

"Sarah!" Mary sounded scared. "Thee aren't going to talk to that officer? Besides, what would thy father say if he found out. He told us to go straight to my house."

"Mary, don't be silly. This will only take me a second. Wait here for me."

"But Sarah, look! He's going inside."

"I've got to find out about Thomas," said Sarah. "Hold my books. I'll be right back," and Sarah ran across Arch Street and followed the officer into the inn.

It was dark inside the crowded inn. For a second, Sarah couldn't see. Then she saw the officer talking to the innkeeper. She took a deep breath and walked over to him.

"Excuse me, sir," said Sarah.

The officer paid no attention.

"Excuse me, sir," said Sarah in a loud voice.

The officer stopped talking.

"Well?" he looked down at Sarah.

"Please, sir, I wonder if thee could tell me how to find out the names of men wounded at Brandywine Creek?"

"Well, now, why would a quiet little Quaker girl want to know a thing like that?"

"Well, sir . . ."

"Captain Sandford, at your service," he tipped his hat.

"Well, Captain Sandford, someone I know was fighting there and I want to find out if he got hurt."

"Let's see. To get those names, you'd have to go to all the hospitals in Philadelphia. I'm sure each one has a list of the wounded in their care."

Sarah must have looked unhappy at this news, because the officer then said, "If you'll give me the name, perhaps I can find out for you."

"I thank thee, Captain Sandford, but I must find out for myself. Good-bye." Sarah ran from the inn and back to where Mary was waiting.

"Did thee find out anything?" Mary asked.

"Yes," answered Sarah. "If I want to find out whether Thomas got hurt, I have to go to all the hospitals in Philadelphia."

"Why, that's out of the question," said Mary. "They've turned all sorts of places into hospitals. They're keeping wounded men in two Presbyterian churches, Corman's Sugar Refinery, even the playhouse. Thee will never find him."

"Mary. . ." Sarah paused. "Never say never to me."

Chapter 7
TOGETHER AGAIN

Boom! Boom! A week had gone by quietly, but today the noise was very loud.

"Where doest thou think they are fighting?" asked Sarah.

"Germantown," answered her father. "It's hard to believe, but Washington must have attacked Howe again, right outside the city."

Sarah turned back to her lesson from Fox's Speller. No one had come into the bakery all morning.

"Sarah!" called her mother. "Come help me with these candles."

Sarah went into the kitchen. Mrs. Miller was pouring hot wax into candle molds.

"Thee, Sarah, keep stirring the wax for me while I pour."

Boom! Boom!

"Ah, what a terrible fight must be going on," said Mrs. Miller. "I hope nothing happens to the Schmidts. They should be bringing wounded men into the city very soon."

"Mary's mother took some soup to the hospital Thursday," said Sarah. "She told us that many men had no beds and there weren't enough medicines."

Mr. Miller came into the kitchen.

"Rebecca. Sarah. I have been thinking about something all week. Already hundreds of soldiers are dying every week from camp fever. And now, with this battle at Germantown, more sick and wounded will be brought into the city. We must all get a smallpox innoculation."

"David!" Mrs. Miller sounded frightened. "Thee can't mean it. Whatever has come over thee?"

"Would thee rather have us all come down with smallpox?"

"But we *will* come down with smallpox," she argued. "And I've heard terrible stories about how people die less than two days after getting their innoculations. They're dangerous!"

"Nonsense, Rebecca. Thee hast been believing too many stories. Now why would Washington order smallpox innoculations for all his men if they were dangerous? He doesn't want his army to die from innoculations."

"I don't care what Washington does," said Mrs. Miller. "His orders don't include me. I feel just fine, and I'm not going to get innoculated."

"Then perhaps thee would like to go with Sarah and me while we get one?" asked the baker.

"Well, only so I can take some food to the soldiers." Mrs. Miller began putting some bread in her basket.

"Come, Sarah, get thy coat. We'll have to walk and it's a cool day," said Mr. Miller.

"And that's another thing," said Mrs. Miller as they began walking down Second Street. "What right did the British have to take thy wagon?"

"The British took everyone's wagon. They said they would pay us three shillings a day rental. Besides, I would rather they take the wagon than rob us of flour."

"Or make us keep a British soldier in the house," added Sarah. "What if we had to feed some stranger every day?"

"He wouldn't get much to eat," said Mrs. Miller. "With no food coming into the city, how do they think we will live through the winter?"

"Many poor people will just go hungry." said Mr. Miller. "The suffering is already terrible."

"Look," said Sarah. "All those fences have been torn down." They were walking along Pine Street past St. Peter's Episcopal Church.

"Why are thee surprised? British troops are staying there, and they use the fences for fuel," said Mr. Miller.

The Millers walked to the Pennsylvania Hospital across an open field. Already, wagonloads of wounded soldiers were being brought from the Battle of Germantown.

A man was standing outside shouting at the drivers. "You'll have to go somewhere else. We're full up. Try the State House. There's doctors over there."

Sarah wanted to cover her ears. The cries of the wounded men sounded terrible.

"Sir," said Mr. Miller. "I understand that we can get a smallpox innoculation here."

"Inside." He jerked his thumb towards the door and the Millers went in.

"Innoculations?" said a man in answer to Mr. Miller. "That room down the hall."

Sarah began to wonder how much it was going to hurt.

"Are thee sure thee won't change thy mind, Mother?" asked Sarah.

Mrs. Miller shook her head. She felt she might faint, the smell was so bad.

Sarah watched her father get his innoculation. There seemed to be nothing to it.

"Are you ready?" the doctor smiled at her.

"Yes," said Sarah and rolled up her sleeve.

Then the doctor took what looked like a large needle and dipped it in some fluid. He took the needle and scratched her arm until the skin broke.

"There you are," said the doctor.

"Is that all there is to it?" asked Sarah.

"Well, you will probably feel like staying in bed for a few days. So just get plenty of rest and don't go outside to play."

Mr. Miller thanked the doctor and paid him.

"We would like to give some bread to the wounded," said Mrs. Miller. "Can thee tell us where to go?"

"End of the hall and turn left," said the doctor. "The soldiers will be happy to see you. We have been very short of food."

The halls were crowded and noisy, but they found their way to a large room. The wounded men were crowded together, some on beds, some even lying on the floor.

Mrs. Miller began at once to give each of the men some bread.

"I pray thee gets well."

"Thee looks good today." Mrs. Miller went from bed to bed.

"Water. Just a bit of water," said a soldier whose cheeks were burning from fever.

Sarah ran for a wet cloth and wiped the soldier's face.

The bread was nearly gone. Mrs. Miller was about to send her husband home for more when she saw a familiar face in the next bed.

"Thomas! Oh, son!" She stood rooted to the floor.

"Oh, Thomas! We found thee." Sarah put her arms around a smiling brother and began to cry.

Mr. Miller stood at the end of the bed. He said nothing.

"Thomas. What happened to thy arm? How long hast thee been here? When did thee get hurt?" Mrs. Miller stroked her son's head.

"One question at a time, please," Thomas laughed. "Howe circled us at Brandywine Creek. I was with Nathanael Greene's men at Chadd's Ford. We had to stop the enemy long enough to let the army retreat. I took a bayonet in the shoulder." He pointed to the dressing on his left arm.

"Then thee hast been here several weeks," said Sarah.

"Since mid-September," answered her brother. "The first week I was here, I had a fever and don't remember anything. Then, when I got better, I couldn't find anyone to take thee a letter. How is everything at the bakery?" He looked at his father.

Still Mr. Miller said nothing to his son.

"Oh, Thomas, everything has changed. For a while, there was no school because Brother Todd would not sign the loyalty oath."

"Well, aren't thee lucky?" laughed Thomas.

"And Thomas." added Mrs. Miller. "There is no salt or butter to be had. Sooner or later we will run out of flour for the bakery."

"Yes, here at the hospital wounded Americans are the last to be fed. If it weren't for the townspeople, we wouldn't have much to eat at all," said Thomas.

"Guess what, Thomas," said Sarah. "The British took our wagon. And before that, the Americans took our blankets. They even took father's winter coat."

Thomas reached for his coat lying at the end of the bed. "Well," he said, "that's easy enough to fix. I surely can't get my coat on, so thee may as well wear it." He held the coat towards his father.

Sarah held her breath. Mr. Miller took the coat.

"I thank thee, son." The baker reached over and took Thomas' hand.

Sarah smiled. The family was together again. It was just like Brother Allen had said at meeting. Love *was* the best rule of all.

EPILOGUE

After Washington lost the Battles of Brandywine and Germantown, he took the American Army to Valley Forge for the winter. While Washington's men nearly starved, the British spent a cozy winter in Philadelphia. Just as Mr. Miller said, the city became very short of food and fuel. Many people went hungry, and hundreds of prisoners died from starvation or sickness.

In June of 1778, the British Army left Philadelphia and Congress returned. The Liberty Bell was moved back to the State House. The city again became the capital of the colonies until 1783.

When the danger was over, the government let the Quaker leaders return to their families. Quaker schools opened again, and Sarah and Mary went on with their studies. Although many Quakers remained neutral during the Revolution, others like Thomas Paine and Thomas Miller joined the American Army. Quakers like Thomas Miller started a new church, called the Society of Free Quakers, who were nicknamed "Fighting Quakers." Sister Griscom's daughter was Betsy Ross, who was said to have made the first American flag.

After the 13 colonies won independence, Philadelphia again became a political center. Delegates from the 13 new states wrote the United States Constitution there in 1787. It was the nation's capital from 1790 to 1800.

Today, a visitor to Philadelphia can see many of the places mentioned in the story—Market Street, the wharfs, the State House, and Betsy Ross' house. In spite of its large crack, the Liberty Bell still reads "Proclaim liberty throughout the land, unto all the inhabitants thereof."

IMPORTANT DATES OF THE REVOLUTION

1775	April 19	Fighting at Lexington and Concord
	May 10	Ethan Allen captures Fort Ticonderoga
	June 15	George Washington elected commander-in-chief of army
	June 16/17	Battle of Bunker (Breed's) Hill
	September	American soldiers invade Canada; Ethan Allen captured
	November/ December	British and Americans fight in Canada, South Carolina, New York, Virginia, Maine, and at sea
1776	March 17	British withdraw from Boston
	July 4	Congress adopts the Declaration of Independence
	August 27	Battle of Long Island; Americans retreat
	September 15	British take New York City
	September 16	Americans win Battle of Harlem Heights
	October 11/13	British fleet wins Battle of Lake Champlain
	October 28	British win at White Plains, N. Y.
	November 16	British take Fort Washington
	November 28	British take Rhode Island
	December	Washington takes army across Delaware and into Pennsylvania
	December 26	Washington wins Battle of Trenton, New Jersey

1777	January 3	Americans win Battle of Princeton
	January	American army winters at Morristown, New Jersey
	August 6	Battle of Oriskany, N. Y.
	August 16	Americans win Battle of Bennington, Vt.
	September 11	British win Battle of Brandywine
	September 26	British occupy Philadelphia
	October 4	British win Battle of Germantown
	October 6	British capture Forts Clinton and Montgomery
	October 7	Battles of Saratoga, N. Y.; British General Burgoyne's army surrenders October 17
	November 15	Articles of Confederation adopted
	December 18	Washington's army winters at Valley Forge
1778	February 6	France signs treaty of alliance with America
	June 18	British evacuate Philadelphia
	June 28	Americans win Battle of Monmouth Court House, N.J.
	July 4	George Rogers Clark wins at Kaskaskia
	August 29	Battle of Rhode Island; Americans retreat
	December 29	British capture Savannah, Ga.
1779	January	British take Vincennes, Ind.
	February 3	British lose at Charles Town
	February 14	Americans win at Kettle Creek, Ga.
	February 20	Americans capture Vincennes
	March 3	British win at Briar Creek, Ga.
	June 20	Americans lose at Stono Ferry, S.C.
	July 16	Americans take Fort Stony Point, N. Y.
	August/ September	Fighting continues on land and sea. On September 23 John Paul Jones captures British *Serapis*
	December	Americans winter at Morristown, N.J.
1780	May 12	Charles Town surrenders to British
	June 20	Battle of Ramsour's Mills, N. C.
	July 30	Battle of Rocky Mount, S. C.
	September 26	Battle of Charlotte, N. C.
	October 7	Battle of King's Mountain, S. C.
1781	January 17	Americans win Battle of Cowpens, S. C.
	March/April	Battles in North Carolina, South Carolina, Virginia, Georgia
	October 19	British army surrenders at Yorktown
1782	July 11	British leave Savannah, Ga.
	November 30	Preliminary peace signed between America and Britain
	December 14	British leave Charleston, S. C.
1783	September 3	Final peace treaty signed
	November 25	British evacuate New York City

About the Authors:

Susan Dye Lee has been writing professionally since she graduated from college in 1961. Working with the Social Studies Curriculum Center at Northwestern University, she has created course materials in American studies. Ms. Lee has also co-authored a text on Latin America and Canada, written case studies in legal history for the Law in American Society Project, and developed a teacher's guide for tapes that explore women's role in America's past. The writer credits her students for many of her ideas. Currently, she is doing research for her history dissertation on the Women's Christian Temperance Union for Northwestern University. In her free moments, Susan Lee enjoys traveling, playing the piano, and welcoming friends to "Highland Cove," the summer cottage she and her husband, John, share.

John R. Lee enjoys a prolific career as a writer, teacher, and outdoorsman. After receiving his doctorate in social studies at Stanford, Dr. Lee came to Northwestern University's School of Education, where he advises student teachers and directs graduates in training. A versatile writer, Dr. Lee has co-authored the Scott-Foresman social studies textbooks for primary-age children. In addition, he has worked on the production of 50 films and over 100 filmstrips. His biographical film on Helen Keller received a 1970 Venice Film Festival award. His college text, *Teaching Social Studies in the Elementary School*, has recently been published. Besides pro-football, Dr. Lee's passion is his Wisconsin cottage, where he likes to shingle leaky roofs, split wood, and go sailing.

About the Artist:

Richard Wahl, graduate of the Art Center College of Design in Los Angeles, has illustrated a number of magazine articles and booklets. He is a skilled artist and photographer who advocates realistic interpretations of his subjects. He lives with his wife and small son in Evanston, Illinois.